KU-337-213

To Tom McArthur
from his Sunday School Teacher,

Christmas 1931

D 942

"WHERE MAY YOU BE FROM?"

Page 37

Frontispiece

PUT TO THE PROOF

BY

MRS. HENRY CLARKE

Author of "The Mystery of the Manor House"
"Little Miss Vanity" &c.

BLACKIE & SON LIMITED
LONDON AND GLASGOW

BLACKIE & SON LIMITED
50 Old Bailey, London
17 Stanhope Street, Glasgow

BLACKIE & SON (INDIA) LIMITED
Warwick House, Fort Street, Bombay

BLACKIE & SON (CANADA) LIMITED
Toronto

Printed in Great Britain by Blackie & Son, Ltd., Glasgow

Contents

PUT TO THE PROOF

CHAPTER I

The Mail-coach

David lived with his uncle in a little brown cottage right up on the hillside, away from the fishing village and the yellow sands where the fishermen spread their nets to dry. The little house nestled snugly under the brow of the hill, and no glimpse of blue water could be got from its windows; but it was so close to the sea that even on calm nights David could hear from his bed the beating of the surf, and in stormy weather the foam of the breaking waves would be carried over the cliffs by the wind, and settle on the thatch like snow.

It was a capital thing for the garden that the hill rose so steeply behind it, sheltering it from the strong sea-winds. Strawberries grew finely there, on the sunny slope set apart for them, and David's early potatoes and cauliflowers were always the first to appear in the market. Twice a week through the summer, on market-days, the cart would be loaded with garden-stuff, and David and Billy the donkey would set off for the town. The sun would be low before they got back, for the road was a hilly one, and Billy never allowed himself to be hurried. Besides, the little cart would be often as full on the journey home as when they set out. Though David never had to bring back any of his fruit or vegetables, he had all sorts of purchases to make in the town. Mrs. Bearne, who kept the only shop in the village, and sold almost everything, from Dutch cheeses to fish-hooks and sun-bonnets, would often give David quite a long list of things she wanted for her customers; and busy mothers in the scattered cottages along the road would run out as they heard the little cart, to get David to do some errands for them in the town. It was easy to ask David to do anything, his pale little face could smile so pleasantly, and he was so eager to be of service. And though he was such a little lad, he was very careful and sensible, and rarely made mistakes.

You must picture him trudging along in the dust one summer evening, leading Billy by the bridle. There was a long hill before them, and David was eager to get to the top. At the top the quiet country road crossed the great highway between Exeter and Plymouth, and he always tried to be in time to see the mail-coach pass. Railways had not been thought of in those days, over a hundred years ago.

Billy sometimes was stubborn, and insisted on cropping thistles by the wayside instead of steadily plodding on, but to-night he was in one of his most amiable moods. David reached the top of the hill some moments before he heard the clear note of the guard's horn that told him the coach had passed Deepleigh Bridge, and was about to appear in sight round the turn of the road.

It came up the hill in fine style, the hoofs of the four horses ringing on the hard road. David watched it with delight; though he had seen it so often it was still a wonderful sight to him. There were spots of foam on the sides of the horses; the coach had been a minute behind time at the bridge, and they were making it up.

As it passed the cross-roads, the guard put his horn to his lips again and blew a friendly note, and some of the passengers looked kindly down on the little fair-haired lad with a donkey-cart, whom the guard and coachman seemed to know.

But in a flash they had passed, and were descending the hill at a gallop, the coach swaying from side to side. Half-way down the hill there was a little dark wood of fir trees. Just as the coach came opposite this wood, David saw a man with a black mask on jump up from behind the stone wall that divided it from the road. He had a pistol in his hand, and he fired at one of the horses. Almost before the sound of the pistol-shot died away, or David knew what was happening, the wounded horse fell, and half a dozen masked men sprang out of the wood.

There were more pistol-shots, a piercing scream or two in a woman's voice, and then a man rushed up the hill towards David, the blood streaming freely from a wound in his forehead. Farther down the hill the highway-

men had already been beaten off, and were
going as fast as they could into the wood, carry-
ing their wounded with them. But David did
not see that; he was staring with pale cheeks
at the blood-stained man coming towards him.
It was the friendly guard.

" Run, run!" he cried to David. " Run to
the bridge for help. I'll go the other way.
We'll have them yet."

David turned and ran. But all his life the
sight of blood had made him feel faint and
sick, and he stumbled as he ran. On one side
of the road there was a deep grassy ditch, full
of water in winter, but now quite dry. Brambles
grew along the top of the ditch, and stretched
long branches into the road. About half-way
down the hill David caught his foot in one of
these branches, and, too dizzy to save himself,
fell forwards and rolled to the bottom of the
ditch, striking his head against a hard lump of
earth. The blow made him faint in real earnest,
and he knew nothing more for a time. When
he opened his eyes again he was propped up
against the bank on the opposite side of the
road, and Mr. Mudge, who kept the turnpike
at the bridge, was bending over him.

"There, there, that's right," he said with rough kindness, as David opened his eyes. "You'll be better now. Don't be scared. They're clean gone, every single one of 'em." And as David stared at him without answering, he turned to a tall man who stood close by, and whispered: "He's the best little chap in the world, sergeant, and as sharp as a needle. But he's more like a girl than a boy. I dare say he thought he wasn't safe, even in the ditch."

The whisper was a loud one, and David heard every word.

"I fell in," he said faintly.

He saw Mr. Mudge grin at the sergeant, but he answered him in the soothing voice he would have used to a timid little girl.

"That's all right. Now, you see if you can stand, and we'll make Billy drive you home. Here's Sergeant Day wants to speak to you. He knew your father and your uncle too."

"That I did," said the sergeant heartily. "Your father and I fought side by side many a time. And I've a letter for your uncle which I was going to send to him from Plymouth when I got a chance. But it's an ill wind that blows nobody any good. I'll give the letter to you, my lad. It's from your Aunt Gracie in Exeter."

The sergeant was a big man with a deep, strong voice. He had keen blue eyes that could look very fierce under his bushy grey eyebrows, but had a very kind, pitying look in them now as he gazed down at David. David knew what he was thinking; he had seen the same thoughts so often in his uncle's kind eyes. He was sorry for him for being so small and pale and weakly. He was thinking it was a sad thing that the only son of a hero should be more like a girl than a boy. David wanted to tell him that it was not fright only which had made him faint; that he had really fallen into the ditch instead of hiding himself there. But he had no time to tell him, even if he could have found the courage.

A man came running up to say that another horse had been found, and the coach was on the point of starting. The sergeant pulled out the letter and gave it to David.

"You and your uncle must come to Plymouth while I'm there, laddie," he said, as he shook him heartily by the hand. "You'll find they remember your father still in the old regiment. But I must be off. His Majesty's mails wait for nobody."

Mr. Mudge helped David to the top of the hill and made him get into the cart. He noticed the big bruise at the back of his head, but treated it very lightly. "You mustn't mind a bit of a knock like that, my boy. Why, when that Tommy of mine fell off the apple tree and broke his arm, he only laughed at the doctor. Now get home and have some supper. Those rascals are far enough off by this time. And they wouldn't touch you anyway. They aren't common roadside thieves. It's a gang that's heard of the gold that is being sent to Plymouth to be shipped. You mark my words, Dave, this won't be the last time they'll try to rob the mail."

David's uncle was still at work in the garden when David got home. He worked very slowly, for he had only one arm; he lost the other fighting against the French in Spain. If their neighbours in the village had not been always ready to lend a helping hand at the busy seasons, the garden could not have looked as it did, though David toiled early and late at it on the days he did not go to market.

Mrs. Bearne, who liked to have her say about everything, told her customers sometimes that Peter Eliot ought to go to market, and David stay at home. But, brave old soldier as Peter was, and fine as he looked on Sundays with his empty sleeve pinned across his breast and all his medals on, Billy could not be taught to respect him, and the cart would never have got to market at all if David had not gone with it. Billy was a donkey who would have but one master, and was not too obedient to him.

It was not till they were sitting at supper in the cosy kitchen that David told his uncle about the letter Sergeant Day had given him. Mr. Eliot did not read the letter at once. He was still too much excited about the highwaymen and David's meeting with the sergeant.

"We'll go to Plymouth, Davie," he said, putting the letter down on the table, and looking at David with his kind eyes. "When Farmer Churchward sends his wagon he'll give us a lift. And we'll tell the sergeant you were obeying orders in running to the bridge. You were on dispatch duty, you see."

"But why did I tumble into the ditch and faint like that?" cried David, who could not forget his fall. "No wonder Mr. Mudge believed I was hiding away. It's quite true what he said; I ought to have been a girl."

"Tut, tut, Davie, I don't like to hear such talk," his uncle answered. "Nobody can help a fall. And you can't make yourself as big and strong as Tommy Mudge for all your trying. We are as God made us. Tommy has not got your brains. He shall do the fighting, and you shall do the thinking; that's fair, isn't it? Now get me my spectacles and we'll see what Aunt Gracie has got to say."

David brought the spectacles, and sat down to listen to the letter. But his heart was very sore. That he was cleverer at books and sums than any boy in the village did not comfort him a bit. He would rather have been stupid Tommy Mudge, able to bear pain so well that he could laugh while the doctor set his broken arm. Uncle Peter might have been proud of him then.

It took his uncle some time to read Aunt Gracie's letter, even with his spectacles on. But at last he put the broad sheet down on the table, and looked at David with a smile.

"Aunt Gracie is giving up her house, Davie.

The colonel and Mrs. Dacre have come back from India, and she is going to live with them again. And she wants Dick to live with us. How would you like that?"

It took David's breath away to think of it. Dick was Aunt Gracie's nephew. His father was a sailor, and Dick had been one or two voyages himself.

"His father won't be back till near Christmas," Peter Eliot went on. "He can stay with us till then, and perhaps after that. He'll be able to help in the garden, and go to market sometimes. Why, it will be first-rate to have him here—eh, Davie?"

"He could not get Billy to market," said David quickly. "I shall have to go too, I'm thinking."

"Well, well, perhaps so. But I'm glad he's coming, Davie. He's a big lad for his age, your aunt says. You'll be able to take things easy."

David squared his shoulders and tried to look twice as big as he was.

"I don't want to take things easy," he said. "And he'll know nothing about the garden or anything."

His uncle looked at him over his spectacles. " Why, David, don't you want him to come?"

David was really eager for Dick to come. He longed to see him, and to hear about his travels. He told his uncle so. But he wished— oh, how he wished!—that he could have behaved that afternoon as Dick would have done. And when he went to bed that night it was to dream that he and the sergeant had followed the masked highwaymen to a secret hiding-place among the cliffs, and made prisoners of them all.

CHAPTER II

On the Cliffs

Dick did not come by the stage-coach; that would have cost too much money. He got a seat in the carrier's heavy wagon, which went from Exeter to Plymouth once a week, and David met him at the cross-roads with Billy and the cart.

Dick was always quick to make friends, and it took him quite a long time to say good-bye to the carrier and the other people in the wagon. They all seemed sorry to lose him, and David did not wonder at it. It was a pleasure just to look at Dick. He was a tall boy, some inches taller than David, though he was a year younger. He had a frank, handsome face, tanned by the sun and wind, and the brightest blue eyes David had ever seen. He was not a bit shy, and as they walked home through the quiet country lanes he did most of the talking. He said the women in the wagon had been watching the hedges all the way from Exeter, for fear masked highway-men should suddenly spring up from behind them. He seemed to be sorry that the journey had been such a peaceful one.

When he heard that David had seen the attack on the coach, his blue eyes grew very bright.

" I wish I had been there!" he cried. " I wish I had been there!"

But he did not go on to question David, for which David was glad. He told him instead a wonderful story of a fight his father's ship once had with a Chinese pirate. He himself was not on board, but David felt quite sure, as he listened to the story, that if he had been, any number of pirates would not have made him afraid.

When they reached the foot of the last long hill they had to climb, Dick wanted to get on faster. He cut a stick from the hedge with his big pocket-knife, and tried by a few smart blows on his fat sides to make Billy know that he must hurry on. But Billy stood stock-still, thrusting out his fore-feet, and looking sideways with stubborn eyes. It was only when

Dick dropped behind, out of sight, that David could get him to move. For Billy was both lazy and self-willed.

" But I'll master him yet," Dick cried. " He's the master now, Dave; that's plain enough. You leave him to me a bit and we'll see what happens."

David looked doubtful. " Uncle Peter can't make him go," he said. " Billy's used to me."

" Oh, I'll make him go!" returned Dick, with a laughing nod. " You shall see when I've been here a little while. And I won't hit him too hard either."

But when they reached the top of the hill Dick was quite content to allow Billy to rest a bit.

Before them lay a fine view of the coast and the wide blue sea. Dick drew a long breath of delight as he looked at the sea. He had loved it all his life. A good way below them lay the little village and the cove with its glistening yellow sands, and on the opposite hill was the little brown cottage, with its long sunny garden.

" There's no garden about here like it," David said with pride. " And that field below goes with it. But that's no good except for Billy."

"It would make a fine potato field," said Dick, who, as David had already found out, liked to give advice. "I'll dig it up for you. There's plenty of hard work in that," and he stretched out his right arm for David to feel its muscles.

"It's almost as hard as Dad's. You should see my dad, Dave. He's the biggest man in the ship, and the strongest. But strength isn't everything," he added quickly, as he glanced at David. "The strongest man in the world, I've heard Dad often say, would be nothing but a bully and a coward, if he hadn't something better than strength. It's good to hear Dad talk, I can tell you."

It was good to see Dick's face when he talked of his father, his eyes had such a proud, loving look in them.

As they went down the hill at last, he asked the names of the bays and headlands they could see along the coast. What took his fancy most, however, was a line of cliffs to the westward.

It was the wildest bit of the coast for many

miles, David told him. There had been a path round the cliffs once, but it was all broken away. "And from Deadman's Point to Winnicombe Beach it is all quicksands. Nobody goes near them. But there's a way across, old Isaac Lee taught me how to find it. I'll show you, Dick, some day."

"And we'll get round those cliffs," answered Dick. "They are like the cliffs at Portreath, Dave. But the coast is all like that down there, splendid! You'd like it tremendously, I can tell you."

David, who could never look over the top of a cliff without getting dizzy, and hated climbing, did not know how to answer this. But Dick was too fond of talking to notice his silence. And he was eager to tell David how his father had once saved a whole boat's crew, by climbing down the face of a great cliff with a rope.

A few days after Dick came, the two boys started for their first long walk along the coast.

"Take care of Davie, Dick," Uncle Peter called after them from the garden gate. "No breakneck climbing, mind."

"Uncle Peter is as bad as Aunt Gracie,"

declared Dick, as they went down the hill.
" She was always thinking I should be brought
home to her on a shutter with all my bones
broken. I tell you what I want to do, Dave.
I didn't say anything to Uncle Peter for fear
he'd say you mustn't go. I want to get across
the cliffs to that beach—Winnicombe Beach,
isn't it? I was talking to Jim Bearne yesterday,
and he says it's easy enough if you're careful
and keep a cool head. He's been across scores
of times."

David's pale face flushed up. He felt he
would rather run the chance of broken bones
than confess to Dick that he was afraid of the
cliffs. " Oh, it's easy enough," he said in a
careless voice, putting his hands deep into his
pockets just as Dick did. " We shall have
plenty of time to get across."

Dick did not notice David's change of colour.
He took it for granted that all boys loved
climbing as much as he did. And though Uncle
Peter had talked to him a little about David
not being as strong as other boys, he just
thought his uncle was like Aunt Grace, over-
careful.

The way to the cliffs was over the hill on

which the cottage was built, and along a wide stretch of sandy shore to Deadman's Point. Close to the Point a rough cart-road came down to the shore. It joined the high-road at the top of the valley, David said, and was used by the farmers to get sea-weed from the beach, and the fine white sand in the cove beyond the Point.

They could see the cove when they had climbed the path which led to the cliffs. It was a fairy-like place, snugly shut in on three sides by tall pointed rocks, and paved with white sand.

" We must have some of that for the rockery," cried Dick, who was already full of plans for the garden. " We'll bring the cart down and get a load. It's the very thing I wanted."

" Billy doesn't like the beach," David said. His eyes were on the narrow path before them as he spoke. It was cut along the cliffs, steep rocks above, steep rocks below.

Dick was looking at the wide bay beyond the cove; the tide was out, and there were long tracts of sand over which white-winged gulls dipped and flew. There were no nets spread to dry, no boats drawn up, no barefooted children running along the shore.

" It's the quicksands," David said, when Dick asked why it was so lonely. " Nobody comes here. If you got caught you'd sink down and down and never be seen again. Why, ships have been buried here, Isaac Lee used to tell me. He lived in a little house on Winnicombe Beach, and nobody knew the place like he did. He taught me a safe path. I've been many a time with him. Come down and I'll take you right across, Dick."

But Dick wanted to go by the cliffs. They could come back by the sands, he said. And when David said that the tide would be in by that time, he still refused to put off his climb. It would be a stiff bit of work, he could see that, and a walk across those flat sands seemed too tame and easy. He did not know how terribly dangerous the quicksands were, or how very few people could find their way safely across them.

" Come along, Dave!" he cried. " I'll go first; you just follow me."

For some distance the path, though narrow, was a fairly good one, and David got along by clinging to the rough edges of the rocks and looking steadily in front of him. But then came a sharp corner where the path was broken away. Dick was out of sight round the corner. " It's all right here, Dave," he cried. " Make two steps of it."

But David did not answer. He was clinging to the face of the cliff, his cheeks deadly white, his eyes fixed on the sands far below him. He was turning giddy; he felt that in a moment he must fall.

" Dick, Dick!" he cried in a piercing voice.

The next moment Dick was back at his side, holding him tight by the shoulder. " Why, Dave, you aren't afraid!" he exclaimed. And then, as he looked more closely at him, he saw that he was hardly able to stand. " Here, come back," he added. " Why, what a baby you are! But I'll teach you to climb like a monkey before I've done with you. My word, a pretty sailor you'd make!"

He was leading David back along the path all the time he was speaking, and his tone was kind though rough. But David felt that he had lost Dick's respect for ever. And when they got back to the grassy slope that led to the shore, he flung himself down and burst into tears. He knew it would make Dick still more ashamed of him, but he could not help it. His heart felt broken.

Dick stood staring at him, his blue eyes full of wonder and something like disgust. He had been taught to think it shameful for a boy to cry. Tears were for girls.

But after a moment he sat down by David, and put his hand on his shoulder. And there was no roughness in his voice now.

" Dave, old chap, it was all my fault. I ought to have seen you couldn't do it. You haven't got the head for it."

David sat up, dashing the tears from his eyes. This new gentleness of Dick's was harder to bear than his roughness. " My head turns like a top when I look down a high place," he said, speaking very fast. "I can't help it. If your head went round like a top you couldn't climb, Dick?"

" Of course I couldn't," Dick answered, still speaking in a gentle voice. " You should have told me, Davie. Why didn't you?"

" Because I was ashamed to," David burst out; and before Dick could answer there came a loud shout from the top of the cliff. It was Tommy Mudge. He was waving his hat and calling to them.

" I'll find out what he wants," cried Dick, guessing that David would not like his red eyelids to be seen.

He was off up the hill in a moment, and was soon back again.

" Davie, there's an old sailor over at Winnicombe Beach who's making a boat for Tommy. He lives just at the bottom of the cliffs, Tommy says."

David looked up. " There's nobody living near the beach," he said. " Isaac Lee used to live there, but he died last year, and his cottage got unroofed in the winter."

" Then the roof must be on again," said Dick quickly, " for that is where the sailor is living —in Isaac Lee's house. Tommy said so. I'd like very much to see the boat, Dave. Couldn't you go round by the sands and meet us at the beach?"

" The tide's come in too far," David answered, trying his best to speak in a cheerful voice. " I couldn't get round the Point. I'll wait here, Dick."

Dick did not go at once. Then the thought of the boat, and his longing to get across the cliffs, proved too much for him. " I'll be back in no time, you see, Dave," he cried, and was off to join Tommy.

Long after they were out of sight David could hear them calling merrily to each other. He tried to feel glad that Dick should enjoy his climb after all, but it was very hard to be glad.

CHAPTER III

Caught by the Tide

It was just about a week after that that Uncle Peter came home from the village one evening with startling news. The bank in the market-town had been broken into the night before, and a large amount of gold carried off. No trace of the thieves had yet been found, but soldiers were coming from Plymouth to help in the search and guard the neighbourhood. It was thought that a large gang of thieves must be hidden somewhere along the coast.

Dick longed with all his heart to go off with Tommy Mudge next day to meet the soldiers, but he could not go, he knew. He had already spent two or three merry evenings with Tommy, scrambling over the cliffs, and talking to the old sailor on Winnicombe Beach. He must stick to his work in the garden all next day. David was going, as he had gone every year since he was a little chap, to help Farmer Churchward's daughters pick the cherries from their wonderful white-heart cherry tree, which was known for miles around.

Farmer Churchward's daughters were very fond of David, and a day at the farm had always been a great treat to him. But this time he did not enjoy it as much as usual. He had been very dull all the week. Though Dick, each time he went out, had asked him to come, promising to keep away from the cliffs, David had known that he was glad to go without him. And David had looked forward so eagerly to long walks with Dick. Though he could not climb, he knew the shore better than any boy in the village, and could have shown Dick all its wonders: the deep caves under the cliffs; the pools where star-like anemones, blue and purple and pink, were to be found; the path across the quicksands. He felt it very hard that Dick should want Tommy Mudge for a friend instead of him.

It was about seven o'clock when David got back from the farm. He had a basket of good things: a pot of clotted cream, and another of strawberry jam, besides butter and eggs, and a large cabbage-leaf full of the precious cherries. He had been thinking, as he climbed the hill, what a fine supper they would have, but when he reached the cottage it was empty. He put the basket down, and then ran to the garden gate to watch for his uncle and Dick. A woman from the village passed as he stood there. She told him that his uncle had gone that afternoon to the coastguard station to see Lieutenant Mayne, and was not yet back. But she knew nothing about Dick.

After talking to her a little, David went up the garden again, and it was then he found out that Dick had taken Billy and the cart. And he thought of what Dick had said about the sand in the cove beyond Deadman's Point. Dick had been at work on the rockery that afternoon, David could see that. He must have gone to fetch some sand, so that he might finish it.

David glanced at the sun, and then set off running as fast as he could over the hill.

The tide was coming in. It would be high tide at sunset. Long before that, the sands round Deadman's Point would be under water.

When David got down to the shore, he knew that he had been right in thinking that Dick had gone to the cove. There, on the yellow sand, were the prints of Billy's hoofs and the marks of the cart-wheels, a little deeper at some places than others, as though Billy had stood still there, refusing to move.

David ran quickly on, keeping his eyes fixed on the tide. It was a calm, bright evening, and the sea was all a shining blue, just streaked with white where the waves ran up the sand. But the tide was coming in very fast; when David reached the Point he had to take off his shoes and stockings to wade round it. The waves broke very gently over his feet, but he knew that in a little while the sandy shore just here would be under deep water. And not even Dick could climb the steep cliffs above him!

Before he got round the Point, he could hear Dick's voice, now in coaxing tones, now in angry ones. David knew what was the matter. Billy had turned stubborn and refused to move. He ran on, shouting Dick's name as hard as he could.

Dick did not hear him. He was on the other side of the little cove, close to the rocks. He had filled the little cart with the white sand, and been ready to start home nearly an hour before.

But nothing would persuade Billy to go round the Point again. He had a curious fear and dislike of the sea, and would not go near it. In vain Dick tugged at his bridle, gave him smart blows on his sleek hide with the stick he carried, scolded and coaxed by turns. Billy would not move, and the tide crept steadily up towards the Point.

Dick made up his mind at last to empty the cart; perhaps Billy would move then. But the instant he let go Billy's bridle and moved towards the back of the cart, the donkey flung up its head and trotted off round the rocks towards Winnicombe Beach.

Dick was thankful to see it move; it had stood as if its feet were fixed in the ground like the roots of a tree. He let it go, but a glance at the tide made him hurry after. When David reached the little cove, he was just in time to see Dick going round the opposite point.

David never forgot that moment. Beyond those rocks the quicksands began.

" Dick, Dick!" he shouted as loud as he could, as he ran on. And then again: " Dick, Dick!"

Dick heard that time. He ran back, wondering what had frightened David, and how he had found out where he and Billy had gone. There was a merry smile on his face as he ran round the rocks; he was ready to tell David that if he had dragged Billy to the cove, he could not get him home again. But when he saw David, his own face turned white.

"Dave, what's the matter?" he cried. "We can get back all right, can't we?"

David caught hold of his arm. "The quicksands!" he panted out.

He started off running again, and Dick turned and ran at his side.

"Billy's close by," he said. "Wait a minute, Dave; I'll go on. He won't have gone far."

"The quicksands!" David panted out again.

In another moment they were beyond the rocks, and then Dick knew what David meant. Where they stood the sand was firm, but a few steps farther it ceased to be so. A yard or two from them poor Billy was struggling to gain a footing, while sinking farther and farther down in the soft sand.

"Dave, what's to be done?" Dick cried.

He made a step forward, but David held him back. And he felt himself that his strength would not help him if once his feet were caught in those cruel sands.

"What's to be done?" he cried again, without any hope in his voice. "Can't we do anything?"

David had been thinking. His brain was quicker than Dick's, and he saw a way of saving poor Billy. Before Dick knew what he was going to do, he ran back a few steps, and then with a flying jump or two, hardly touching the sand with his feet, he was in the cart. It sank a little deeper beneath him, but only a little. It is useful to be small sometimes.

"Dick, throw me your big knife," he called.

Dick obeyed. David was the leader now, and spoke like one. In an instant he had the knife open, and was cutting away the harness. At the sound of his voice, so near at hand, Billy ceased to plunge and kick, though he was still trembling all over. David cut the reins and knotted them together, and then turned to Dick and flung one end to him. It just fell within his reach. Then followed the most trying part of the rescue. It was a long time before they could get Billy clear of the cart, and every moment was precious.

But neither of the lads thought of leaving Billy to his fate while there was any chance of saving him. And after a long struggle Billy was got back to firm ground again. The cart had to be left; it was a great loss, but there was no help for it.

But neither of the boys gave a thought to the cart as they hurried across the wide bay to Winnicombe Beach. There was just time to reach the beach before the tide stopped them, David said. It was lucky that Isaac Lee had taught him a safe path through the quick-sands, for they could not have got round the point. The water was now nine feet deep there, and more, dashing high against the rocks.

As they came near the line of low rocks which hid Winnicombe Beach from them, they thought they heard the sound of men's voices.

" Tommy's friend has a party," said Dick, who had got back his good spirits again. " There's never been a soul here before."

As he spoke, the old sailor who was making a boat for Tommy Mudge appeared in the narrow passage between the rocks. He was a short, thick-set man, with a brown face, and gold rings in his ears. David did not like the

look of him, nor the sound of his hoarse voice.
But he did not speak for a moment. He stared
at the two boys and the donkey, as if not able
to believe his own eyes.

" Where may you be come from?" he asked,
after looking them up and down. " Dropped
from the skies, maybe?"

He listened to their story, and asked them a
great many questions, but he did not move from
the rock. He was not very hospitable, David
thought. Isaac Lee would have had them up
to the hut at once, and given them food and
drink, the best he had.

He turned to David presently, looking down
at him from under his bushy eyebrows.

" I reckon you're a clever little chap, sonny.
Now this path you're talking of, can you teach
it to an old sea-salt like me? It'll save my old
bones a bit if I can cross the sands instead of
going round by the road."

" I'd be glad to show you," David answered,
looking timidly up at him. " But nobody could
learn it by going across once or so. There's lots
of things to think of."

Hawkins nodded. " But you can think of 'em.
What a thing it is to have your head screwed

on the right way, sonny! You come again to see old Hawkins. He's taken a fancy to you, he has."

" Couldn't he stay the night with you, Mr. Hawkins?" broke in Dick. " It's six miles by the road if it's an inch, and I don't believe he can walk it."

" I can," cried David stoutly. He felt he would rather spend the night by the wayside than stay alone with Mr. Hawkins, who, indeed, did not seem eager to ask him to be his guest. " It's five miles to the town, and I walk there twice a week."

" Because Billy is a lazy beast," said Dick, with a laugh. " If he wasn't too old and stupid, I'd teach him better manners. He's dead lame to-night or he should carry you home. It's the least he could do, for you saved his life, and mine too." Dick added the last words with a flush, and a look which made David feel very happy.

" You want a pony, sonny," said the old sailor, " that's what you want. There's one laying up for you now, maybe. Don't forget old Hawkins said it. But if you're going by the road, I'll walk along with you a bit. It's a

lonely place I've got here, not a living soul
have I set eyes on to-day."

" But I'm sure I heard voices," David declared some time after, when Hawkins had gone
back to the hut, and they were trudging along
the country road under the quiet evening sky.
" Didn't you hear them, Dick?"

" It must have been the waves on the beach,"
Dick replied. " Hawkins says there are all sorts
of queer noises on that beach at night. I'm
glad you didn't stay there, after all. Isn't he a
regular old sea-salt, Dave?"

" He isn't like the sailors I've known, not
very much," said David, shaking his head. He
did not like Mr. Hawkins.

Dick burst into a laugh, and put his arm
round David's shoulders. Though he felt as
strongly as a generous-hearted boy could feel
what he owed to David, he still looked on him
as very much weaker and more timid than himself, and therefore to be pitied and taken care
of.

" Yes, I'm glad you didn't stay, Dave. You'd
have been frightened at the tales Hawkins tells;
he's had a rough life of it. But he's a fine old
fellow. Dad would like to know him."

David did not answer this. They were hailed just then by a man in a wagon, who had just turned the corner of the road behind them. He offered them a lift, which the boys were glad to accept. He was only going as far as Winnicombe, the big, straggling village half-way along the road, but even that was a great help. David was ready to confess afterwards that he could not have got home at all without it.

CHAPTER IV

A Midnight Summons

Uncle Peter had not come back when the tired and hungry boys reached home. The fire was almost out, and the only cheerful greeting that awaited them was from the basket on the little round table, from which the cherries in the cabbage-leaf peeped out beside the pot of yellow cream.

They were too hungry to wait for their uncle, and after David had given Billy his supper, and Dick had kindled the fire on the hearth afresh, stirring the peat ashes and casting on sticks till a ruddy blaze went up, they sat down to the little feast Miss Churchward had provided.

Dick did full justice to the good things, but David soon found that he was too tired to eat much. And when, after supper, he sat down on his three-legged stool by the fire, he fell fast asleep almost at once, his head resting against the corner of his uncle's cushioned arm-chair.

It was quite dark when he woke up at last, except for the dancing firelight. His uncle had come home, and was seated at the table eating his supper. David sat up slowly and rubbed his eyes.

" Why, I've been asleep!" he remarked, in a tone of such surprise that Dick and his uncle burst out laughing.

" I should think you have been asleep," cried Dick. " Why, Uncle Peter's been home an hour and more. I've been telling him all about it. Dad will buy us a new cart when he comes home, Dave. Uncle Peter says he can borrow one till then. But Billy's very lame, Uncle Peter. You and Dave must wish I'd never come here. What an idiot I was to go off like that! But for Dave there, where should I be now?" Dick's voice trembled as he spoke, and there were tears in his eyes. But he was not going to let them be seen. He jumped up to get Uncle Peter his pipe from the chimney-piece. " Dave ought to go to bed, Uncle Peter. I'll carry you up if you'll let me, Dave. I'm sure I could."

" I'm sure you couldn't," said David sharply, " and you aren't going to be allowed to try, either." And then he wondered at himself for being cross with Dick. " I don't want to go to bed yet," he said, sitting up very straight. " I'm not tired a bit."

" You'll be tired enough to-morrow, Davie, unless I'm much mistaken," said his uncle in a very kind voice.

Though he was more vexed at the loss of the cart than he had allowed Dick to guess, it had made his heart warm to know what a wise little chap David had proved himself that afternoon.

It was not his way to openly praise or blame, but the very sound of his voice told David how much he was pleased. And the two exchanged a very loving glance before David spoke again.

" I'd rather stay up a bit longer," he said. " Did you see Lieutenant Mayne, Uncle Peter?"

" Yes; I had to wait, though. He was over at Squire Truscott's when I got there. He wants the squire to send all his silver and her ladyship's jewels to Plymouth to be taken care of. But the old squire just laughed heartily at him. He doesn't in the least believe this story about a gang of land-pirates hidden along the coast. He told the lieutenant about a man named Falstaff, who mistook one thief for ten."

" But you know that I saw them, Uncle," said David, with a flush.

" So you did, laddie. But the squire wouldn't believe his own eyes, the lieutenant says, if they saw a thing that he'd made up his mind couldn't be seen. The lieutenant thinks the thieves have got a ship that runs in at night and takes them off. But he hasn't seen a sign of her."

" Hawkins said the very same thing to me, Uncle Peter," said Dick; " he's on the watch too. Winnicombe Beach would have been the very place for them if he wasn't there. What were you going to say, Dave?"

For David had given a little start, as if some strange thought had suddenly come into his head.

" David's half-asleep," his uncle said, smiling at him. " Off to bed, boys. No more talking, Dick."

" But have the soldiers come, Uncle Peter?

I wish it was market-day to-morrow," cried Dick.

" It's no good thinking about market till we've got another cart, young man," said his uncle gravely. And then, fearing he had been too severe, he added: " Yes, the soldiers have come. And what do you think, Davie, Sergeant Day is with them. The lieutenant told me so this afternoon. He'll be over here before he goes back."

David felt no great desire to see Sergeant Day again. The memory of their last meeting was still a painful one. But Dick was full of eagerness at the news.

" I can't be as sorry about the cart as I ought to be," he said to David, when they had climbed the ladder to their little room under the thatch, " my head's full of the soldiers now. Uncle Peter thinks I don't care, I know. But I do care, only I can't help thinking of the soldiers. Wouldn't it be fine, Dave, if you and I could see a real fight? I'd take care of you. I wish we could go and help the soldiers in the search to-morrow. Old Hawkins and Tommy are going. But there are those potatoes to dig. But " duty first and pleasure afterwards ", as

Dad says. I wish I had thought of that this afternoon."

But Dick was not to dig potatoes for very long next day. Just after dinner, which they always had at twelve o'clock on working days, Lieutenant Mayne, the bluff, red-faced, coast-guard officer, a great friend of David's, drove up to the garden gate in his little trap. He made no move to descend, however.

Dick was busily digging potatoes at the bottom of the garden; Uncle Peter was comfortably smoking his after-dinner pipe by the kitchen hearth, so it was David who heard the lieutenant's cheery shout. He ran at once to the gate. He was off to the town, the lieutenant told him, and thought his uncle might like to go too.

" I've heard that a party of these rascals mean to land at Thurston Cove to-night, ten miles down the coast. We'll be ready for them. But call your uncle, David, call your uncle; I've no time to waste. Don't expect him back before morning."

David was going to the house, but the lieutenant called him back again.

" Would you like to go too, David? I've

just room to squeeze you in.   But perhaps you'd better not."

David looked up eagerly.

" Please, lieutenant, couldn't Dick go?"

" Dick? That's your cousin, isn't it? Well, we'll think about it."

" Do take him, sir," pleaded David.

" See what your uncle says," replied the lieutenant, with a laugh. " You don't mind being left at home alone, then?"

David replied that he did not mind a bit, but he found that he had to say this over and over again before he could make his uncle and Dick believe it.

" I'll get Jim Bearne to come up," Uncle Peter said, when he found that David really wanted Dick to go.

David could have burst into tears at this suggestion.

" I don't want Jim or anybody," he said, squaring his shoulders and looking quite fierce. " What is there to be afraid of?"

So Uncle Peter and Dick drove away with Lieutenant Mayne, and David stood at the gate and waved his cap to them till they were out of sight.

Dick's heart smote him when he saw the little figure at the gate.

" I think I'll go back, Uncle Peter," he said suddenly.

" Nonsense, nonsense!" exclaimed the lieutenant. " I'm taking you to please David, and you'll have to go." He turned to Dick's uncle and added: " David's just as well at home, Eliot. We may have to wait all night at Thurston Cove. It's the morning coach they're after, Hawkins says."

Dick gave a start at this.

" Did old Hawkins tell you, sir?" he asked eagerly.

The lieutenant looked vexed.

" Yes, he did," he said shortly. " But no blabbing, mind. I did not mean to mention him. He got the information from somebody at Thurston, whose name he wouldn't tell me. And he doesn't want his own name mixed up in it. So keep a still tongue in your head, youngster."

Dick felt snubbed, and it was not for a good many hours afterwards, when they were waiting behind the rocks at Thurston Cove, that he told the lieutenant of the voices he and David had heard on Winnicombe Beach.

The day passed cheerfully at the cottage. Jim Bearne came in for an hour, and brought David some currant buns from his mother. But he did not offer to stay the night; his father's boat was going out soon after sunset with the rest of the fishing fleet. He looked at Billy's foot, which was badly swollen, and shook his head over it. It would want a long rest, he said.

David was low-spirited for a little while after Jim went away, wondering how they were to get on without Billy and the cart. But he was soon cheerful again. He felt sure they would manage somehow. He ate his buns for supper, and then did a little more digging at the potatoes till it was too dark to see.

The house seemed very quiet when he went in. As he sat in the kitchen he could hear quite well the rush of the waves. It was high tide, and they were breaking against the foot of the cliffs on the other side of the hill. The waves had always had a friendly voice to him before, but to-night he did not care to listen. He did not tell himself that he was afraid, but he felt that it was time to go to bed. He raked the ashes carefully over the fire on the hearth, and then slowly climbed up the ladder to his room. He felt much less lonely when he had said his prayers, and was snug in bed under the patchwork quilt. In a very few moments he was sound asleep.

It was dark when he fell asleep, as dark as summer nights ever are. When he awoke, the moon had risen and was shining through the little window in the roof. He started up suddenly, thinking he had heard Dick call him. And then he knew that Dick was not in the room with him, nor in the house.

But someone was calling him. David sat up in bed and listened. He had left the kitchen door unbolted, as his uncle always did, and somebody was standing at the foot of the ladder calling him. He knew the voice. It was Tommy Mudge's. He jumped out of bed and went to the top of the ladder.

" Tommy, is that you?"

" Yes," returned Tommy. His voice was hoarse. " Dress and come down, David. You are wanted."

David began to tremble. " Nothing's happened to Uncle Peter or Dick, has there?" he asked faintly.

" No, they're all right. Come down, David. Mr. Hawkins wants you. He told me to say so. Do be quick and come. There's nothing to be frightened at. But you're wanted."

CHAPTER V

Conclusion

David dressed as quickly as he could, and ran down the ladder. Then he found that Tommy was not alone. A man David had never seen before, dressed like a fisherman in a blue-knitted jersey and oil-skin cap, was standing close by him.

The kitchen door stood wide open, and the moonlight came in. David could see that Tommy was as pale as death and shaking all over; even his teeth were chattering. It alarmed David dreadfully to see that Tommy was frightened. But the man did not give him time to ask more questions. He was holding Tommy by the arm, and he now caught hold of David's arm, and hurried them out of the cottage.

" You'll soon be snug in bed again, sonny," he said to David in a voice he tried to make soft and friendly, but which had a very alarming sound in David's ears. " Tell him it's all right," he added more roughly, giving Tommy a little shake.

" It's all right," Tommy said, with chattering teeth. " It's all right, David."

But as he spoke he was looking wildly from side to side, as if watching for some means to escape, and his words only served to frighten David more than ever.

They had now crossed the brow of the hill, and could look down on the moonlit sea and the wide sandy shore. Far out to sea the sails of some big ship showed white in the moonlight, but except for that the sea was as lonely as the shore. The fishing fleet had sailed from the little harbour some hours ago, and was now half-way to Plymouth. The tide was going out, there was already a strip of sand round the point.

The man stopped for an instant or two, as if waiting for some signal. But all was silent, except for the low ripple of the waves on the sand. And from end to end of the wide shore no moving thing was in sight. He began to hurry on without speaking, but that pause had given David a little courage. He tried to drag himself out of the man's grasp.

" Where is it you're taking me?" he cried. " I'm not going on till I know. Tommy, you tell me."

The sailor stopped again, looking down at David with a sort of amused surprise in his face, as if a little bird had flown at him. " Oh, you won't go on, eh?" he said, with a big laugh. " Hark to that, Tommy! Why, you are a lad of spirit, you are!" At that moment a cry, like the note of a sea-bird, came over the sands, and at once his manner changed. " But stop this nonsense and come along," he growled roughly. " Nobody's going to eat you, if that's what you are afraid of. You're in for a bit of good luck, sonny. You'll be coming back this way before morning with a handful of golden guineas in your pocket."

He was hurrying them down the grassy slope as he spoke. Away across the sands David could just see a group of dark figures coming down the rough cart-track, which joined the high-road at the top of the valley.

" Step out, my lads," the sailor exclaimed, as he hurried on still faster. " Some folks get vexed if they're kept waiting. And they'll be there before us now."

The dark figures moved swiftly along, keeping in the shadow of the rocks. There were about a dozen in all, more than half of them with heavy bundles on their backs. And all in a moment David knew who they were, and what they wanted him for. They were the robbers he had seen attacking the mail-coach, and they meant to make him lead them across the quick-sands!

Tommy had not spoken since they left the hillside, and David could not have spoken now if he had wanted to. The sailor was hurrying him along so fast that there was no breath left in his body. When at last they got round the point into the cove, and his arm was released, he staggered back against the rocks unable to stand upright.

No one took any notice of him for a moment or two. The old sailor whom the boys had known as Hawkins, and who appeared to be the leader of the band, spoke sharply to the men, telling them to take up their sacks again, which they had put down on the sand. And Tommy, with a sharp cry, sprang towards a tall man standing between two others with his hands tied behind his back. It was his father. Mr. Mudge had been crossing some lonely fields at the back of the turnpike on his way home from the town when he fell in with the robbers, who were coming from Squire Truscott's with their spoil. And they had brought him to the cove with them for fear that he should give an alarm. He fixed a stern, reproachful glance on his son, and Tommy burst into tears.

"Father, I couldn't help it," he sobbed out. "They made me do it."

Hawkins, who was standing close by, turned sharp round at this.

"That's just so," he said, putting his great knotted hand on Tommy's shoulder, and chuckling as the boy shrank away from him. "Don't you go blaming Tommy, Mr. Mudge. When old Hawkins says a thing's to be done, it has to be done. And now if little Dave has got his breath again we'll start. And when we're safe on the other side, Dave can bring you and Tommy back again. A nice little party you'll be. Why, I wish I could come back with you. Come along, little Dave; you and me will go first. Come along, sonny; old Hawkins is in a hurry to-night. Don't you keep him waiting."

David made no answer. He was leaning back against the rocks, staring hard at the old sailor's smiling face. He was horribly frightened, but he did not move. Hawkins thought he was too frightened to move. He went on in a coaxing voice: " Just you come along with old Hawkins, sonny. Nobody's going to hurt you, not a bit of it. It's going to be money in your pocket. Why, in half an hour or so you'll be back again with Mr. Mudge and Tommy. Tommy isn't such a clever lad as you, I wouldn't trust him to lead us. But you come along with me—come along, now."

David braced his shoulders against the rock. He was deadly pale, but his eyes had a steady light in them. He remembered his father—his father who had died with his face to the foe.

" I won't do it," he said, stammering a little, for his lips were trembling, but looking straight into the old sailor's face.

Hawkins stared at him for a moment, and then caught him roughly by the arm. " March!" he said in a tone of thunder. " Come, lads, follow me!"

He half-led, half-dragged David to the other side of the cove and round the low rocks. But there he stopped. Before him lay the quick-sands, divided here and there with lines of water that shone in the moonlight. Without David for a guide, he was afraid to move another step.

He thrust David on before him. "March!" he ordered again, in the same thundering voice.

David turned round and faced him, his small hands clenched at his sides. He was frightened, terribly frightened, but he never thought of giving way. There was the soul of a hero in his small frame.

"I won't do it," he stammered out again.

For answer, Hawkins struck him a blow across the face which sent him staggering to his knees, but the next instant the old sailor caught him by the arm and dragged him to his feet again.

"You be a good boy and do what old Hawkins tells you to," he said. He thrust his hand into his pocket and pulled out a little bag of soft leather tied round with string. He held it up before David. "There's money in it, golden guineas, all ready for you. Put it in your pocket, nobody need know. It'll be a little fortune for you, sonny."

He pushed the bag into David's hands, but it fell on the ground. David had been half-stunned with the blow, but now his weakness seemed suddenly to leave him. He looked Hawkins boldly in the face.

" I wouldn't take your money," he said. " And I won't lead you across the sands. You can't make me do it."

" We'll see about that, my lad," returned the old sailor, with a wicked look. " We'll see about that."

He snatched a great knife from his belt, and David shrank back with a faint cry, as he saw it glitter in the moonlight.

" Right-about-face, march!" ordered the old sailor. " Be quick about it, too."

But David did not move.

" I won't," he said. " You may kill me if you like, but I won't do it."

At that moment a shrill whistle rang out from behind the rocks, where one of the men had stayed as guard. Hawkins rushed back, and the others after him, taking Mr. Mudge with them. Tommy ran up to David, and the two boys clung together, wondering what the whistle meant. They were not long left in doubt.

There was a rush of feet along the sands, the clash of weapons.

"Surrender, in the king's name!" rang out a clear, strong voice.

"Davie, Davie, it's the soldiers!" gasped out Tommy, hugging David in his joy. "And but for you they would have been too late!"

It was the soldiers, headed by Sergeant Day and the lieutenant. At Thurston Cove Dick had told Lieutenant Mayne of the strange voices on Winnicombe Beach, and he had told the sergeant. It made them think that Hawkins had sent them to Thurston Cove to get them out of the way. They had ridden hard back again, to hear that Squire Truscott's had been visited, and all the silver and jewels carried off. They had followed the thieves at once, but as Tommy truly said, if it had not been for David's courage they would have been too late.

The struggle in the cove was only a short one. All the thieves were taken prisoner and marched off to the town, and soldiers were set to guard the silver till a cart could be sent to

fetch it. Then Lieutenant Mayne and the
sergeant heard from Mr. Mudge how it was
that they had found the thieves in the cove,
instead of half-way across the quicksands, safe
from pursuit. Mr. Mudge was a just man, and
though he wished it had been Tommy who had
played the brave part, he made them under-
stand what a little hero David had proved himself.

Sergeant Day was a man of few words, and
when he went to speak to David he did not
say as much to him as Lieutenant Mayne. But
the words he did say were the sweetest David
had ever heard. He put his hand on his shoulder,
looking down at him with his keen eyes.

" You are your father's son, my lad. He
would have been proud of you this day."

. . . .

Some days afterwards David and Dick were
busy in the garden, late in the afternoon. It
was market-day next day, and they were getting
ready for it. Billy was too lame to go, it was
feared that he would never be fit for much
again; but Farmer Churchward had promised
to lend them a pony and cart till harvest began,
though after that he would not be able to do so.

" We must have a cart and horse of our own before next year," Dick said, digging hard at the potatoes. " Now that Squire Truscott has given you those fields, Dave, we can make a fine thing of the garden."

For the day before Squire Truscott and his wife, Lady Laura, had called at the cottage, and brought with them a parchment deed from the lawyers, which said that the two fields next to the garden were to be David's very own, to do what he pleased with. And Dick had never stopped making plans about the garden since.

" But if you go away to sea, Dick, how would Uncle Peter and I get on?" said David, who was picking peas close by, and stopped to speak before going down the row again.

" We'll make Dad buy a boat and live with us," said Dick, with an eager laugh. " He has often talked of it, and he'd like it here, I know. Then I could go fishing half the time, and help you the other half, like Jim Bearne. And Tommy's a capital hand for work if you tell him exactly what to do. We'll have him to help. But there's Uncle Peter calling us. What does he want, I wonder?"

Dick put down his hoe and went up the

garden. David followed with the basket of peas in his hand. Their uncle met them, his kind face full of excitement and pleasure.

" Come to the gate, David, there is something for you to see. And you come too, Dick."

Wondering what it was they were to see, the boys followed their uncle to the gate. There stood a beautiful little market-cart, painted green, drawn by a stout black pony, whose new harness glittered in the sun. Jim Bearne had just driven it up to the gate and left it there. Tied to the pony's bridle was a large card, on on which was written, " For David Eliot, from his friends ".

" It's yours, Davie," his uncle said. " Look at the writing. And there is your name painted in full on the cart, ' David Eliot '. I knew it was coming, Lieutenant Mayne told me so. Isn't it a beauty?"

David stared at the cart and then at his uncle. Then his eyes went back to the cart again, and at last fixed themselves on the black pony, who was already regarding him with a very friendly look.

" Mine!" he gasped.

It seemed too good to be true.

Dick dashed open the gate and ran out to bring the pony in.

" Hurrah!" he cried. " You need never walk to market again, Dave. The pony's a beauty, and so is the cart. But they aren't a bit too good for you, and that everybody knows."